Enid Blyton's

Mr Grumpgroo's H

ILLUSTRATED BY HELEN SMITH

A TEMPLAR BOOK

Produced by The Templar Company plc, Pippbrook Mill, London Road, Dorking, Surrey RH4 1JE, Great Britain.

Text copyright © *Mr Grumpygroo's Hat* 1953 by Darrell Waters Limited
This edition illustration and design copyright © 1996 by The Templar Company plc
Enid Blyton's signature mark is a registered trademark of Darrell Waters Limited

This edition produced for Parragon Books, Units 13-17, Avonbridge Trading Estate, Atlantic Road, Avonmouth, Bristol BS11 9QD

This book contains material first published in My Second Enid Blyton Book by Latimer House 1953.

Printed and bound in Great Britain

ISBN 0-75251-441-5

Mr Grumpygroo was the crossest old man in the whole of Tweedle village. No one had ever seen him smile, or heard him laugh. He was so mean that he saved all his crumbs and made them into a pudding instead of giving them to the birds.

Of course, everyone was a little frightened of Mr Grumpygroo. They kept out of his way and the children hid if they saw him coming. He didn't seem to mind. He lived all alone in his tumbledown cottage, and made friends with no one.

But really Mr Grumpygroo was very lonely. He often wished the children would smile at him as they smiled at the other villagers. But they never did, and old Grumpygroo vowed that he wouldn't be the first to smile at anyone, not he!

Every day he went walking through the village with his old green scarf round his neck and his battered brown hat on his head, leaning heavily on his walking stick.

He might have gone on scowling and frowning for ever, if something strange hadn't happened. One morning he went into the hall to fetch his scarf and his hat. It was rather a dark day, and old Grumpygroo could hardly see. He felt about for his scarf, and tied it round his neck. Then he groped about for his hat.

There was a lamp standing in the hall on the old chest where Mr Grumpygroo usually stood his hat. On it was a lampshade made of yellow silk with a fringe of coloured beads. By mistake Mr Grumpygroo took up the shade instead of his hat, and it was so dark that he didn't see the mistake he had made. He put the lampshade on his head! It felt rather like his old brown battered hat, so he didn't notice any difference; and out he walked into the street!

He looked very funny indeed, walking along with a lampshade on his head. All the beads shook as he walked. As he went out of his gate the sun came out, the birds began to sing, and it turned into a lovely spring day.

Even old Mr Grumpygroo felt a little bit glad, and he half wished he had a friend who would smile at him. But he knew nobody would, so he set his face into a scowl, and went down the street.

The first person he met was the jolly Balloon woman carrying her load of balloons. When she saw the yellow lampshade on his head, she smiled, for he looked so very funny.

Grumpygroo thought she was smiling at him, as he didn't know what he had on his head, and he was most surprised. He didn't smile back, but went on his way, wondering why the balloon woman had looked so friendly for the first time in ten years.

The next person he met was Mr Plod, the village policeman, who loved a joke. When he saw the lampshade perched on old Grumpygroo's head, he grinned very broadly indeed.

Mr Grumpygroo
blinked in surprise. Could
it be the fine spring morning that
was making people so friendly?

"I shall smile back at the very next person who smiles at me," said Grumpygroo to himself, feeling quite excited. "If people are going to be friendly, I don't mind being nice too."

Round the corner he met Mr Macdonald the farmer riding on his old horse. As soon as the farmer caught sight of the lampshade, he smiled so widely that his mouth almost reached his ears.

And so Mr Grumpygroo smiled back! Old Macdonald nearly fell off his horse with astonishment, for he had ever seen such a thing before! He ambled on, lost in surprise, and Grumpygroo went on his way with a funny warm feeling round his heart.

"I've smiled at someone!" he said to himself. "I've forgotten how nice it was. I hope someone else smiles at me, for I wouldn't mind doing it a second time."

Four little children came running up the street. As soon as they saw Mr Grumpygroo with the yellow lampshade on his head, they forgot to run and hide as they usually did. Instead, they smiled and laughed in delight.

Mr Grumpygroo was so pleased. He smiled too, and the ice round his heart melted a little bit more. He was starting to enjoy this strange new feeling.

The children laughed merrily and one of them put her hand in his, for she thought Grumpygroo had put the lampshade on to amuse her.

Something funny happened inside Mr Grumpygroo then. He wanted to sing and dance. It was lovely to have people so friendly towards him.

The next person he met was Mr Crumb, the baker. Mr Grumpygroo smiled at him before Mr Crumb had time to smile first. The baker was so surprised that he nearly dropped the load of new-made cakes he was carrying. Then he saw Grumpygroo's lampshade hat, and he gave a deep chuckle. Grumpygroo was delighted to see him so friendly.

"Good morning," he said to Mr Crumb. "It's a wonderful day, isn't it?"

The baker nodded his head and laughed again.

"Yes," he said; "and that's a wonderful hat you're wearing, Mr Grumpygroo."

Grumpygroo went on, very much pleased.

"What a nice fellow to admire my old hat," he thought. "Dear me, and I always thought the people of this village were so unpleasant. That just shows how mistaken I can be!"

He smiled at everyone he met, and everyone smiled back, wondering why Grumpygroo wore such a funny thing on his head. By the time he reached home again, he was quite a different man. He smiled and hummed a little tune, and he even did a little jig when he got into his front garden. He was so happy to think that people had been friendly to him.

"It shows I can't be
as grumpy and cross
as they thought I was,"
he said to himself. "Well,
well, I'll show them what a fine
man I am. I'll give a grand party,
and invite everyone in the village to
it. Whatever will they say to that!"

He walked into his hall, and was just going to take off his hat when he saw himself in the mirror. He stood and stared in surprise – whatever *had* he got on his head!

"Oh my, oh my, it's the lampshade!" he groaned, and he took it off. "Fancy going out in that! And oh dear! Everyone smiled at the lampshade, because it looked so funny – they didn't smile at *me* after all!"

How upset Grumpygroo was! "How dreadful to have to wear a lampshade on my head before people will smile at me!" he groaned. "I must be a most unpleasant old man. Well, I will just have to show people that I've changed. I had better organise my party right away. Perhaps the village folk will learn to smile at me for myself if I'm nice to them. I'll send out those party invitations at once!"

He did – and wasn't everybody surprised!

The party was a great success, everyone had a wonderful time and soon old Grumpygroo had heaps of friends. Nobody could imagine what had changed the old fellow and made him so nice, nor could anyone understand why he kept his old yellow lampshade so carefully on display, long after it was dirty and torn.

But Mr Grumpygroo knew why!
It had brought him smiles and
plenty of friends – but he wasn't
going to tell anyone that – not he!